The Man That Corrupted Hadleyburg

A Scathing Satire of Morality,
Temptation & the Hypocrisy of
Honest Folk

A Modern Translation
Adapted for the Contemporary Reader

Mark Twain

Translated by Tim Zengerink

Table of Contents

Preface
Message to the Reader

Rebuilding the Greatest Library in Human History

Thousands of years ago, the Library of Alexandria was the heart of global knowledge — a sanctuary where the wisdom of every known civilization was gathered and shared freely.

And then, it was lost.

Now, we're rebuilding it — and you are invited to join us.

At the Library of Alexandria, we've set out to make every book available to every person on Earth — not just in print, but in every language, every format, and for every reader.

Here's how we do it:

- **Deluxe Print Editions at True Printing Cost** - Order any book as a high-quality paperback, elegant hardcover, or stunning boxset — and only pay what it costs to print. No markups. No middlemen.
- **Unlimited Access to the Greatest Works** - Enjoy thousands of timeless classics — from Plato to Shakespeare to Tolstoy — in beautiful, modern eBook and audiobook editions. Read and listen without limits — for every reader, everywhere.
- **Modern Translations for Every Language & Dialect** - We're reimagining the classics in clear, accessible language — and translating them into every dialect imaginable. Everyone deserves to understand humanity's greatest ideas.

When you visit **LibraryofAlexandria.com**, you're not just accessing books — you're joining a global movement to restore, preserve, and share the wisdom of civilization.

Join us today at LibraryofAlexandria.com

Together, we'll ensure the light of human wisdom never fades again.

With gratitude,

The Modern Library of Alexandria Team

Visit:
www.libraryofalexandria.com
Or scan the code below:

Introduction

Mark Twain's Satirical Masterpiece and Its Place in Literary History

Among the many works of Mark Twain, *The Man That Corrupted Hadleyburg* stands out as a brilliant, biting satire that unflinchingly examines the moral pretensions of individuals and the collective hypocrisy of a self-righteous community. Written in 1899 during a period when Twain's own outlook on humanity had grown increasingly dark and skeptical, this novella represents one of his most searing commentaries on the nature of virtue, greed, and human fallibility. It is not merely a story about one fictional town and its downfall but also a universal reflection on how easily even the most "honest" societies can be led astray by temptation, vanity, and the desire for social validation.

The novella was first published in *Harper's Monthly Magazine* and later included in a 1900 collection. It arrived at a time when Twain was grappling with personal tragedies, financial troubles, and a growing disillusionment with the societal values of the late 19th century. This historical backdrop provides important insight into the tone and themes of the story. Unlike the light-hearted humor that characterizes earlier Twain works such as The Adventures of *Tom Sawyer* or *Adventures of Huckleberry Finn*, *The Man That Corrupted Hadleyburg* is charged with a much darker humor— sarcastic, ironic, and at times almost caustic. The laughter it provokes often has a sting, for it emerges from an uncomfortable recognition of universal human weaknesses.

The town of Hadleyburg is portrayed as a community obsessed with its reputation for incorruptibility and moral purity. Its citizens take pride in their ability to resist temptation, boasting about their unshakeable virtue. However, Twain cleverly constructs a scenario where this very reputation becomes their undoing. The arrival of a mysterious stranger and the promise of a sack of gold quickly reveal the superficiality of Hadleyburg's moral foundation. What follows is not only a story of collective downfall but also a profound commentary on the dangers of self-deception, moral arrogance, and the corrupting influence of greed.

Mark Twain's narrative style in this work is both sharp and deliberate. He uses a detached yet penetrating voice, often highlighting the absurdity of human behavior by juxtaposing lofty ideals with petty actions. While the novella is relatively short compared to his major novels, its brevity does not diminish its impact. Every scene is infused with purpose, serving both the plot and the broader moral critique. For modern readers, this story resonates just as powerfully as it did over a century ago, for the themes Twain addresses—hypocrisy, moral posturing, and societal corruption—remain deeply relevant.

The story also reflects Twain's broader philosophical shift during his later years. While earlier works often celebrated individualism, freedom, and moral courage, *The Man That Corrupted Hadleyburg* takes a more cynical stance on human nature. It suggests that virtue is not an inherent quality but rather a fragile construct, easily shattered when placed under the right pressures. Through the character of the stranger and the reactions of Hadleyburg's citizens, Twain illustrates how quickly people abandon their principles when faced with the lure of wealth or the fear of public humiliation.

In addition to its thematic richness, the novella is notable for its structural precision. Twain wastes no time establishing the central conflict and quickly sets in motion a series of events that escalate the tension and expose the duplicity of each character. The story unfolds like a carefully crafted moral parable, with each twist of the plot serving to deepen the satire. The climactic revelation of the townspeople's hypocrisy, followed by the eventual collapse of Hadleyburg's reputation, delivers a satisfying yet unsettling conclusion. Twain does not offer redemption or moral resolution; instead, he leaves readers with a lingering sense of discomfort, urging them to question their own assumptions about integrity and virtue.

Twain's language in *The Man That Corrupted Hadleyburg* is as precise and cutting as a scalpel. His wit, while often humorous, also functions as a powerful tool for critique. Consider, for example, his descriptions of the townspeople's self-congratulation, which border on the absurd. By exaggerating their moral pride, Twain underscores the inherent flaws in any community that claims moral superiority. This technique—using humor to expose serious truths—has long been one of Twain's trademarks, but in this novella, it is particularly potent.

Moreover, the story raises important questions about the nature of honesty and corruption. Is corruption an external force, as the people of Hadleyburg seem to believe, or does it arise from within? Twain's narrative suggests that the seeds of corruption are always present, waiting for the right conditions to flourish. The stranger's role in the story is not so much that of a villain but rather that of a catalyst, revealing what already lies hidden in the hearts of the townspeople. This nuanced perspective adds depth to the story and challenges readers to reflect on their own moral assumptions.

Themes, Motifs, and the Universality of Twain's Message

One of the central themes of *The Man That Corrupted Hadleyburg* is the fragility of human virtue. Twain invites readers to question whether true incorruptibility exists or whether it is merely a façade maintained by favorable circumstances. The citizens of Hadleyburg are proud of their reputation, but their supposed integrity has never truly been tested. When temptation arrives, their moral posturing crumbles with astonishing speed. This theme is timeless, for every society, regardless of era or culture, faces the tension between public image and private morality.

Another prominent theme is the destructive power of greed. The sack of gold introduced by the stranger becomes a symbol of both temptation and exposure. It serves as a mirror, reflecting the true nature of each character. The frantic attempts of Hadleyburg's leading citizens to claim the gold reveal not only their personal selfishness but also the broader moral bankruptcy of the community. Twain's treatment of this theme is both humorous and unsettling. While readers may laugh at the absurdity of the characters' behavior, they are also forced to confront the uncomfortable truth that greed is a universal human impulse.

Hypocrisy, too, lies at the heart of the novella. Twain is merciless in his portrayal of Hadleyburg's leaders, who outwardly profess high moral standards while secretly scheming to gain wealth and power. The town's downfall is not caused by external corruption but by the duplicity and vanity of its own people. This critique extends beyond the fictional setting of Hadleyburg, pointing to the broader tendency of societies to elevate hollow moral ideals while failing to uphold them in practice. Twain's satire thus transcends its immediate context, offering a biting commentary on human nature itself.

The stranger, whose identity remains largely mysterious, functions as both a plot device and a moral agent. His scheme to expose Hadleyburg's hypocrisy is not motivated by greed but by a desire for revenge and justice. In this sense, he serves as a kind of antihero, challenging the complacency and arrogance of the townspeople. Through the stranger, Twain explores the idea that moral reckoning often comes from unexpected sources. His character raises difficult questions about whether exposing corruption justifies acts of deception or manipulation.

Another key motif in the novella is the concept of reputation. Hadleyburg's citizens are obsessed with how they are perceived, both by outsiders and by one another. Their sense of self-worth is tied not to genuine virtue but to public recognition. When their reputation is threatened, they resort to desperate measures to preserve it. Twain's critique of this obsession with appearances is particularly relevant in today's world, where social status and public image often overshadow authentic moral character.

In addition to its themes, the novella is rich with symbols. The sack of gold, for instance, is not merely a plot device but a symbol of temptation, power, and moral testing. It is the catalyst that forces the townspeople to reveal their true selves. Similarly, the public reading of the letters that supposedly identify the rightful owner of the gold serves as a metaphor for public scrutiny and judgment. These symbols enhance the story's depth and invite readers to consider the broader implications of the narrative.

Twain's prose style in *The Man That Corrupted Hadleyburg* is particularly effective in conveying these themes and motifs. His use of irony, hyperbole, and sharp dialogue brings the characters to life while simultaneously exposing their flaws. The humor in the story, while often dark, serves a dual purpose: it entertains while also prompting critical reflection. Twain's ability to balance these elements is one of the reasons why the novella remains a masterpiece of American literature.

For readers approaching this work for the first time, it is helpful to keep in mind the historical and cultural context in which it was written. At the turn of the 20th century, America was undergoing significant social and economic changes. Industrialization, urbanization, and the rise of new wealth were transforming traditional values. Twain, who had witnessed the corruption and excesses of the Gilded Age, sought to challenge the myth of moral superiority that many communities claimed. *The Man That Corrupted Hadleyburg* can thus be read as both a specific critique of his contemporary society and a universal meditation on the flaws of human nature.

As you embark on this reading journey, consider how Twain's satire applies not only to the fictional town of Hadleyburg but also to modern communities, institutions, and individuals. The story's enduring relevance lies in its ability to provoke self-examination. Who among us can truly claim incorruptibility? How do our own societies balance the tension between public image and private morality? These questions, which Twain raises with such sharp wit and insight, remain as urgent today as they were more than a century ago.

In conclusion, *The Man That Corrupted Hadleyburg* is not just a story—it is a moral mirror. Twain challenges readers to look beyond surface appearances and confront the uncomfortable truths about human behavior. His satire, while often humorous, cuts to the core of what it means to be virtuous, honest, and true. As you read this novella, allow yourself to be both entertained and challenged. Pay close attention to Twain's language, his use of irony, and the ways in which he constructs his moral critique. Doing so will not only enhance your appreciation of this masterpiece but also deepen your understanding of the timeless human struggles it portrays.

Chapter I.

This happened many years ago. Hadleyburg was the most honest and upright town in the entire surrounding region. The town had maintained that spotless reputation for three generations and took more pride in it than any of its other achievements. The community was so proud of this distinction, and so determined to ensure it would continue, that it started teaching principles of honest conduct to babies while they were still in their cradles, making these lessons the foundation of their education throughout all their school years. During their formative years, temptations were deliberately kept away from young people, allowing their honesty to strengthen and become deeply ingrained, becoming part of their very nature. The surrounding towns envied this honorable distinction and pretended to mock Hadleyburg's pride in it, dismissing it as mere vanity; however, they were still forced to admit that Hadleyburg was truly an incorruptible community; and when pressed, they would also concede that simply being from Hadleyburg was all the endorsement a young man needed when he left his hometown to look for respectable work.

But eventually, as time passed, Hadleyburg had the misfortune to offend a traveling stranger—perhaps without realizing it, certainly without caring, since Hadleyburg was self-sufficient and didn't give a damn about strangers or what they thought. However, it would have been wise to treat this particular man differently, because he was bitter and vindictive. Throughout his travels over an entire year, he nursed his grievance and spent all his free time trying to devise a fitting revenge. He came up with many schemes, and all of them were solid, but none was comprehensive enough: even the weakest would harm numerous individuals, yet what he sought was a strategy that would encompass the whole town and ensure that not a single person escaped unharmed. Finally, he struck upon a brilliant idea, and when it occurred to him, it filled his entire mind with wicked delight. He immediately began developing his plan, telling himself "This is exactly what I need to do—I will corrupt the town."

Six months later, he traveled to Hadleyburg and arrived at the home of the bank's elderly cashier around ten o'clock at night, riding in a horse-drawn carriage. He pulled a large bag from the carriage, hoisted it onto his shoulder, and struggled with its weight as he made his way through the cottage yard before knocking on the door. A woman's voice called out "Come in," so he entered and placed his bag behind the stove in the living room, speaking courteously to the elderly woman who was sitting by the lamp reading the "Missionary Herald":

"Please stay seated, ma'am, I won't bother you. There— now it's hidden quite well; you'd barely notice it was there. Could I speak with your husband for a moment, ma'am?"

No, he had gone to Brixton and might not come back until morning.

"Very well, madam, it doesn't matter. I simply wanted to leave that bag in his care, to be given to the rightful owner when they are found. I am a stranger; he doesn't know me; I am just passing through the town tonight to take care of something that has been on my mind for a long time. My task is now finished, and I leave feeling pleased and a little proud, and you will never see me again. There is a note attached to the bag that will explain everything. Good night, madam."

The elderly woman felt frightened by the mysterious large stranger and was relieved when he left. However, her curiosity got the better of her, so she walked directly to the sack and retrieved the paper. It started like this:

"TO BE PUBLISHED, or, the right man sought out by private inquiry—either will answer. This sack contains gold coin weighing a hundred and sixty pounds four ounces—"

"Have mercy on us, and the door isn't even locked!"

Mrs. Richards rushed to the door, trembling as she locked it, then quickly pulled down all the window shades and stood there feeling frightened and worried, wondering if there was anything else she could do to make herself and the money safer. She listened for a while, alert for any sounds of burglars, then gave in to her curiosity and returned to the lamp to finish reading the paper:

"I am a foreigner, and I'm currently returning to my own country to stay there for good. I'm thankful to America for everything I've received during my extended time living under her flag; and to one of her citizens—a resident of Hadleyburg—I'm especially thankful for a tremendous act of kindness he showed me a year or two ago. Actually, two tremendous acts of kindness. Let me explain. I was a gambler. I say I WAS. I was a broke gambler. I came to this town at night, starving and without a cent to my name. I asked for help—in the darkness; I was too embarrassed to beg in daylight. I approached the right person. He gave me twenty dollars—which is to say, he gave me life, as I saw it. He also gave me prosperity; because with that money I made myself wealthy at the gambling tables. And lastly, a comment he made to me has stayed with me until this day, and has finally defeated me; and in defeating me has rescued what's left of my moral character: I will gamble no more. Now I have no clue who that person was, but I want him located, and I want him to receive this money, to give away, discard, or keep, however he chooses. It's simply my way of showing my appreciation to him. If I could remain, I would search for him myself; but it doesn't matter, he will be located. This is a trustworthy town, an honest town, and I know I can rely on it without worry. This person can be recognized by the comment he made to me; I'm convinced that he will recall it."

"Here's my plan: If you'd rather handle this investigation privately, go ahead and do that. Share what I've written here with anyone you think might be the person we're looking for. If someone responds by saying, 'I'm the one you're looking for; what I said was such-and-such,' then put them to the test like this: open the bag, and inside you'll discover a sealed envelope that contains those exact words. If what the person claims they said matches what's written in the envelope, give them the money and don't ask any more questions, because that person is definitely who we're searching for."

"But if you would rather have a public investigation, then publish this letter in the local newspaper—along with these instructions: Thirty days from today, the candidate should come to the town hall at eight in the evening on Friday and give his statement, sealed in an envelope, to Reverend Mr. Burgess (if he's willing to help with this); then Mr. Burgess should break the seals on the sack right there, open it, and check whether the statement matches: if it's correct, the money should be given to my benefactor, now properly identified, along with my heartfelt thanks."

Mrs. Richards sat down, trembling slightly with excitement, and soon became absorbed in her thoughts—following this line of thinking: "How strange this all is! ... And what incredible luck for that generous man who cast his bread upon the waters! ... If only it had been my husband who did it!—because we're so poor, so old and poor! ..." Then, with a sigh—"But it wasn't my Edward; no, it wasn't him who gave a stranger twenty dollars. What a shame; I can see that now... " Then, with a shudder—"But this is gambling money! the wages of sin; we couldn't accept it; we couldn't even touch it. I don't want to be anywhere near it; it feels like contamination." She moved to a chair farther away... "I wish Edward would come home and take it to the bank; a thief could break in at any time; it's terrifying to be here all alone with it."

At eleven o'clock, Mr. Richards arrived, and while his wife was expressing "I am so glad you've come!" he was declaring, "I am so exhausted—completely worn out; it is terrible to be poor, and have to make these depressing trips at my age. Always working, working, working, for a salary—another man's servant, and he sits at home in his slippers, wealthy and comfortable."

"I feel so sorry for you, Edward, you know that; but take comfort; we have our way of making a living; we have our good reputation—"

"Yes, Mary, and that's all there is to it. Don't pay attention to what I'm saying—it's just a brief moment of frustration and doesn't mean anything. Kiss me—there, it's completely gone now, and I'm not complaining anymore. What have you been buying? What's in the bag?"

Then his wife revealed the enormous secret to him. It stunned him for a moment; then he said:

"It weighs a hundred and sixty pounds? Why, Mary, that's forty thousand dollars—just think about it—an entire fortune! There aren't even ten men in this village who are worth that much money. Hand me that paper."

He quickly read through it and said:

"What an adventure this is! It's like a romance story; it's like those impossible things you read about in books but never actually see happen in real life." He was completely excited now; cheerful, even joyful. He patted his old wife on the cheek and said with humor, "We're wealthy now, Mary, wealthy; all we need to do is bury the money and burn the papers. If that gambler ever shows up asking questions, we'll just look at him coldly and say: 'What nonsense are you talking about? We've never heard of you or your bag of gold before;' and then he would look like a fool, and—"

"And meanwhile, while you're going on with your jokes, the money is still sitting here, and it's quickly approaching the time when burglars come out."

"That's right. Alright then, what should we do—keep the investigation private? No, not that; it would ruin the excitement. The public approach is better. Think about what a stir it will create! And it will make all the other towns envious; because no outsider would entrust such a matter to any town except Hadleyburg, and they're well aware of it. This is a tremendous advantage for us. I need to get to the printing office now, or I'll be too late."

"But stop—stop—don't leave me here alone with it, Edward!"

But he had already left. However, he wasn't gone for very long. Close to his own home, he encountered the editor who owned the newspaper, handed him the document, and told him, "This will be perfect for you, Cox—publish it."

"It might be too late, Mr. Richards, but I'll take a look."

At home again, he and his wife sat down to discuss this delightful mystery; they were too excited to sleep. The first question was: Who could the townsperson have been who gave the stranger the twenty dollars? It seemed like a straightforward question; both answered it at the same time—

"Barclay Goodson."

"Yes," Richards said, "he could have done it, and it would have been just like him, but there isn't another person in the town who would have."

"Everyone will admit that, Edward—admit it privately, at least. For six months now, the village has returned to being its true self again—honest, narrow-minded, self-righteous, and stingy."

"It is what he always called it, to the day of his death—said it right out publicly, too."

"Yes, and he was hated for it."

"Oh, absolutely; but he didn't care. I think he was the most hated man among us, except for Reverend Burgess."

"Well, Burgess has it coming—he'll never get another congregation in this town. As petty as this place is, people here know exactly what he's worth. Edward, doesn't it strike you as strange that the stranger would choose Burgess to hand out the money?"

"Well, yes—it does. That is—that is—"

"Why so much of that behavior? Would you choose him?"

"Mary, perhaps the stranger understands him better than anyone in this village does."

"That would really help Burgess!"

The husband appeared confused and struggled to find a response; his wife watched him intently and waited. Eventually Richards spoke, with the uncertainty of someone who is about to say something that might be questioned,

"Mary, Burgess is not a bad man."

His wife was definitely surprised.

"Nonsense!" she exclaimed.

"He isn't a bad person. I know this. All of his unpopularity was based on that single incident—the one that caused such a commotion."

"That 'one thing,' indeed! As if that 'one thing' wasn't enough, all by itself."

"Plenty. Plenty. Only he wasn't guilty of it."

"What are you saying! Not guilty of it! Everyone knows he was guilty."

"Mary, I promise you—he was innocent."

"I can't believe it and I don't. How do you know?"

"It is a confession. I am ashamed, but I will make it. I was the only man who knew he was innocent. I could have saved him, and—and—well, you know how the town was worked up—I didn't have the courage to do it. It would have turned everybody against me. I felt terrible, absolutely terrible; but I didn't dare; I didn't have the courage to face that."

Mary appeared upset and remained quiet for some time. Then she spoke hesitantly:

"I—I don't think it would have been right for you to—to—One shouldn't—um—what people think—one has to be so cautious—so—" It was a challenging path to navigate, and she became stuck; but after a moment she found her way again. "It was truly unfortunate, but—Why, we simply couldn't manage it financially, Edward—we really couldn't. Oh, I wouldn't have wanted you to do it for any reason!"

"It would have cost us the goodwill of so many people, Mary; and then—and then—"

"What worries me now is what he thinks of us, Edward."

"He? He has no idea that I could have saved him."

"Oh," the wife exclaimed with relief in her voice, "I'm so glad to hear that. As long as he doesn't realize you could have saved him, he—he—well, that makes everything much better. I should have figured he had no idea, since he's always trying to be friendly with us, despite how little we encourage him. People have teased me about it more than once. There are the Wilsons, the Wilcoxes, and the Harknesses—they get a nasty kick out of saying 'Your friend Burgess' because they know it bothers me. I wish he would stop being so persistent in liking us; I can't understand why he keeps it up."

"I can explain it. It's another confession. When the situation was fresh and heated, and the town planned to run him out on a rail, my conscience bothered me so much that I couldn't bear it, and I went secretly and warned him, and he left town and stayed away until it was safe to return."

"Edward! If the town had discovered it—"

"Don't! It still frightens me just thinking about it. I regretted it the moment I did it, and I was even scared to tell you because your expression might give it away to someone. I couldn't sleep at all that night from worrying about it. But after several days passed, I realized no one was going to suspect me, and then I started feeling happy that I had done it. And I still feel happy about it, Mary— completely and utterly happy."

"I feel the same way now, because it would have been a terrible way to treat him. Yes, I'm relieved; you really did owe him that much, you know. But Edward, what if it comes to light someday!"

"It won't."

"Why?"

"Because everybody thinks it was Goodson."

"Of course they would!"

"Absolutely. And naturally he didn't care at all. They convinced poor old Sawlsberry to go confront him about it, and he went storming over there and did exactly that. Goodson looked him up and down, as if he was searching for the spot on him that he could despise the most; then he said, 'So you're the Committee of Inquiry, are you?' Sawlsberry replied that was pretty much what he was. 'Hmm. Do they want specific details, or do you think a general response will suffice?' 'If they want specifics, I'll return, Mr. Goodson; I'll take the general answer first.' 'Very well then, tell them to go to hell—I figure that's general enough. And I'll offer you some advice, Sawlsberry; when you come back for the details, bring a basket to carry home whatever's left of yourself.'"

"Just like Goodson; it has all the characteristics. He had only one weakness; he believed he could offer advice better than anyone else."

"That resolved the matter and rescued us, Mary. The topic was abandoned."

"Bless you, I'm not doubting that."

Then they returned to discussing the mystery of the gold sack, their interest renewed and intense. Before long, their conversation started to falter—interrupted by periods of deep contemplation. These pauses became increasingly frequent. Eventually, Richards became completely lost in his thoughts. He sat for a long time, staring blankly at the floor, and gradually he began to accompany his thoughts with small, restless hand gestures that seemed to reveal his growing agitation. Meanwhile, his wife had also fallen into pensive silence, and her movements were starting to betray an anxious uneasiness. At last, Richards stood up and began pacing around the room without purpose, running his hands through his hair, much like a sleepwalker might do while caught in a nightmare. Then he appeared to settle on a clear course of action; without saying a word, he grabbed his hat and hurried out of the house. His wife remained sitting there, lost in troubled thoughts with a tense expression on her face, seemingly unaware that she was now alone. Occasionally she whispered, "Lead us not into t... but—but—we are so poor, so poor!... Lead us not into.... Ah, who would be hurt by it?—and no one would ever know.... Lead us...." Her voice trailed off into incoherent murmuring. After a moment, she looked up and muttered in a way that was half-frightened, half-pleased—

"He's gone! But oh no, he might be too late—too late.... Maybe not—maybe there's still time." She stood up and remained there thinking, nervously gripping and releasing her hands. A small tremor ran through her body, and she spoke with a parched throat, "God forgive me—it's terrible to think such thoughts—but.... Lord, how we are created—how strangely we are created!"

She dimmed the light and quietly crept over to kneel beside the sack, running her hands along its bumpy surface and caressing it tenderly; her tired old eyes gleamed with satisfaction. She drifted in and out of distraction, occasionally emerging from her thoughts to whisper "If only we had waited!—oh, if only we had been patient a little longer and not rushed into it!"

Meanwhile, Cox had returned home from his office and told his wife everything about the strange incident that had occurred, and they had discussed it enthusiastically, speculating that the deceased Goodson was the only person in town who could have assisted a suffering stranger with such a generous amount as twenty dollars. Then there was a pause, and the two became contemplative and quiet. And gradually they grew anxious and restless. Finally the wife said, as if speaking to herself,

"Nobody knows this secret except the Richardses... and us... nobody."

The husband snapped out of his thoughts with a small jolt and looked longingly at his wife, whose face had turned very pale. Then he hesitantly stood up and glanced secretly at his hat, then at his wife—a kind of silent question. Mrs. Cox swallowed once or twice, with her hand at her throat, then instead of speaking she nodded her head. In a moment she was alone, and muttering to herself.

Richards and Cox were now rushing through the empty streets from opposite directions. They met at the bottom of the printing office stairs, both out of breath; in the dim glow of the night light, they studied each other's faces. Cox whispered:

"Nobody knows about this except us?"

The whispered answer was:

"Not a single person—I swear, not a single person!"

"If it isn't too late to—"

The men were beginning to climb the stairs when a boy caught up with them, and Cox asked,

"Is that you, Johnny?"

"Yes, sir."

"You don't need to send out the early mail—or any mail for that matter; wait until I give you the word."

"It's already gone, sir."

"Gone?" The word carried the weight of crushing disappointment.

"Yes, sir. The schedule for Brixton and all the towns beyond it changed today, sir—I had to get the papers in twenty minutes earlier than usual. I had to hurry; if I had been two minutes later—"

The men turned around and walked slowly away, not bothering to wait and hear what else would be said. Neither of them said a word for ten minutes; then Cox spoke up in an irritated tone,

"I can't figure out what made you rush like that."

The response was modest enough:

"I understand it now, but somehow I never realized, you know, until it was too late. But the next time—"

"Next time be damned! It won't happen for a thousand years."

The friends parted ways without saying goodnight, dragging themselves home like men who had received a fatal blow. When they arrived at their houses, their wives jumped up eagerly asking "Well?"—but then they saw the answer written on their faces and collapsed in grief without waiting to hear the words. In both homes, heated arguments broke out—something completely new for them. There had been disagreements before, but never angry ones, never harsh ones. Tonight's arguments seemed to mirror each other almost exactly. Mrs. Richards said:

"If you had just waited, Edward—if you had only taken a moment to think; but no, you had to rush straight to the printing office and spread it all over the world."

"It said publish it."

"That doesn't matter; it also said you could do it privately if you wanted to. There, now—is that true, or not?"

"Well, yes—yes, that's true; but when I considered what a commotion it would cause, and what an honor it was to Hadleyburg that a stranger would have such faith in it—"

"Oh, absolutely, I understand all of that; but if you had just taken a moment to think about it, you would have realized that you couldn't possibly locate the right person, because he's dead and buried, and he didn't leave behind any children or family or relatives; and as long as the money went to someone who desperately needed it, and no one would be harmed by it, and—and—"

She broke down and started crying. Her husband tried to think of something comforting to say, and after a moment he came up with this:

"But in the end, Mary, this has to be for the best—it has to be; we know that's true. And we need to remember that it was meant to happen this way—"

"Ordered! Oh, everything's ordered, when someone has to find a way out after they've been foolish. All the same, it was meant for the money to come to us in this particular way, and it was you who decided to interfere with Providence's plans—and who gave you that authority? It was wrong, that's what it was—pure blasphemous arrogance, and completely inappropriate for a humble and modest believer in—"

"But, Mary, you know how we've been raised our entire lives, just like everyone else in the village, until it's become completely natural for us to act immediately without hesitation whenever there's something honest that needs to be done—"

"Oh, I know it, I know it—it's been nothing but endless training and training and training in honesty—honesty that's been protected from the very beginning, shielded from every possible temptation since birth, so it's fake honesty, and it crumbles like nothing when real temptation arrives, as we've witnessed tonight. God knows I never had even the slightest doubt about my rock-solid and unbreakable honesty until this moment—and now, facing the very first major and genuine temptation, I—Edward, I believe this town's honesty is just as corrupt as mine is; just as corrupt as yours. This is a petty town, a harsh, selfish town, and it doesn't possess a single virtue in the world except this honesty it's so famous for and so proud of; and I swear, I truly believe that if the day ever comes when its honesty faces serious temptation, its great reputation will collapse like a house of cards. There, I've confessed now, and I feel relieved; I am a fraud, and I've been one my entire life without realizing it. Don't let anyone call me honest ever again—I won't accept it."

"I—Well, Mary, I feel much the same way you do: I certainly do. It seems strange, too, so very strange. I never could have believed it—never."

A long silence followed; both were lost in thought. Finally, the wife looked up and said:

"I know what you are thinking, Edward."

Richards had the embarrassed expression of someone who had been caught.

"I'm embarrassed to admit this, Mary, but—"

"It doesn't matter, Edward, I was thinking the same thing myself."

"I hope so. State it."

"You were wondering if someone could just figure out what comment Goodson made to that stranger."

"It's absolutely true. I feel guilty and ashamed. And you?"

"I'm done with this. Let's make a bed here; we have to keep watch until the bank vault opens in the morning and lets us get the sack... Oh no, oh no—if only we hadn't made that mistake!"

The bed was prepared, and Mary said:

"The magic words—what could they have been? I really wonder what that comment could have meant. But come on; let's go to bed now."

"And sleep?"

"No; think."

"Yes; think."

By this time the Coxes had also finished their argument and made up, and were going to bed—to think, to think, and turn restlessly, and worry, and agonize over what the comment could possibly have been that Goodson made to the stranded outcast; that precious comment; that comment worth forty thousand dollars in cash.

The village telegraph office stayed open later than usual that night for this reason: The supervisor at Cox's newspaper served as the local correspondent for the Associated Press. You could call him an honorary correspondent, since he rarely managed to submit thirty words that would get published even four times a year. But this situation was different. His message describing what he had discovered received an immediate response:

"Send the whole thing—all the details—twelve hundred words."

A massive order! The foreman was exactly what was needed, and he became the proudest man in the entire state. By the time people sat down for breakfast the next morning, the name of Hadleyburg the Incorruptible was being spoken everywhere across America, from Montreal all the way down to the Gulf, from Alaska's frozen glaciers to Florida's orange groves. Millions upon millions of people were talking about the mysterious stranger and his bag of money, wondering whether the right person would be discovered, and hoping that more news about the situation would arrive soon—immediately, in fact.

Chapter II.

The village of Hadleyburg awakened to find itself world-famous—amazed—joyful—conceited. Conceited beyond belief. Its nineteen leading citizens and their wives walked around shaking hands with one another, glowing with pride, grinning, and offering congratulations, declaring that this event had added a new word to the dictionary—Hadleyburg, meaning incorruptible—destined to remain in dictionaries forever! Meanwhile, the lesser and insignificant citizens and their wives behaved in much the same manner. Everyone rushed to the bank to see the gold sack; and before noon, disappointed and jealous crowds started pouring in from Brixton and all the surrounding towns; and that afternoon and the following day, reporters began arriving from all directions to examine the sack and its story and write the entire tale from scratch, creating bold freehand sketches of the sack, Richards's house, the bank, the Presbyterian church, the Baptist church, the public square, and the town hall where the test would take place and the money would be handed over; along with unflattering portraits of the Richards family, Pinkerton the banker, Cox, the foreman, Reverend Burgess, and the postmaster—and even of Jack Halliday, who was the lazy, good-hearted, worthless, disrespectful fisherman, hunter, friend to boys, friend to stray dogs, and the town's typical "Sam Lawson" character. The small, petty, smirking, slick Pinkerton displayed the sack to everyone who came by, rubbing his smooth palms together with satisfaction, and spoke at length about the town's excellent long-standing reputation for honesty and this remarkable confirmation of it, expressing hope and belief that this example would now spread throughout the

American nation and mark a new era in moral renewal. And so it continued, on and on.

By the end of a week, things had settled down once more; the wild rush of pride and joy had calmed into a gentle, sweet, quiet delight—a kind of profound, indescribable, wordless contentment. Every face showed an expression of serene, sacred happiness.

Then a change occurred. It was a gradual transformation; so gradual that its beginnings were barely noticed; perhaps they weren't noticed at all, except by Jack Halliday, who always observed everything; and always poked fun at it, too, regardless of what it was. He started making teasing comments about people not appearing quite as cheerful as they had a day or two earlier; and then he declared that the new demeanor was deepening into genuine sadness; then, that it was developing a troubled appearance; and finally he stated that everyone had become so brooding, contemplative, and distracted that he could steal a penny from the poorest man in town right out of his pants pocket without interrupting his daydream.

At this point—or around this time—a comment like this would be made at bedtime—typically with a sigh—by the head of each of the nineteen main households:

"Ah, what could Goodson's comment have been?"

And immediately—with a shudder—came this, from the man's wife:

"Oh, don't! What terrible thing are you thinking about? Push it out of your mind, for God's sake!"

But that same question was forced from those men again the following night—and received the identical response. Though weaker this time.

On the third night, the men asked the same question once more—this time with deep pain and distraction. That evening—and the night after—the wives shifted restlessly and weakly, attempting to speak. But they remained silent.

And the night after that, they found their voices and responded—with deep longing:

"Oh, if we could only guess!"

Halliday's remarks became increasingly brilliant in their unpleasantness and criticism with each passing day. He moved about purposefully, mocking the town both as individuals and as a whole. However, his laughter was the sole remaining sound of mirth in the village: it echoed into a hollow and sorrowful void. Not even the faintest smile could be found anywhere. Halliday carried around a cigar box mounted on a tripod, pretending it was a camera, and would stop every person walking by, point the contraption at them, and announce "Ready!—now look pleasant, please," but even this excellent joke failed to coax the gloomy faces into any hint of warmth.

So three weeks went by—only one week remained. It was Saturday evening after dinner. Instead of the usual Saturday night excitement and activity, with people shopping and having fun, the streets were empty and abandoned. Richards and his elderly wife sat separately in their small living room—miserable and lost in thought. This had become their nightly routine: the lifelong habit that came before it, of reading, knitting, and pleasant conversation, or visiting with neighbors or having them over, was dead and gone and forgotten, what felt like ages ago—though it had only been two or three weeks; no one talked anymore, no one read, no one visited—the entire village stayed home, sighing, worrying, silent. Trying to figure out that comment.

The mail carrier delivered a letter. Richards looked without interest at the address and postmark—both unfamiliar—and threw the letter onto the table before returning to his what-if thoughts and his endless, dreary sorrows where he had abandoned them. A few hours later, his wife tiredly stood up and was heading to bed without saying good night—this had become their routine—but she paused near the letter and stared at it for a moment with lifeless curiosity, then tore it open and started scanning through it. Richards, seated there with his chair leaning back against the wall and his chin resting between his knees, heard something drop. It was his wife. He rushed to her side, but she called out:

"Leave me alone, I am too happy. Read the letter—read it!"

He did. He devoured it, his mind spinning. The letter came from a faraway state, and it read:

"I'm a stranger to you, but that doesn't matter: I have something important to tell you. I just got back home from Mexico and learned about what happened. Obviously you don't know who made that comment, but I do, and I'm the only person alive who knows. It was GOODSON. I knew him well many years ago. I was passing through your town that very night and stayed as his guest until the midnight train arrived. I overheard him make that comment to the stranger in the darkness—it happened in Hale Alley. He and I discussed it for the rest of the journey home, and while we were smoking in his house. During our conversation, he mentioned many of your fellow townspeople—most of them in quite unflattering terms, but two or three favorably: you were among the latter. I say 'favorably'—nothing more than that. I remember him saying he didn't actually LIKE anyone in the town—not a single person; but that you—I THINK he said you—I'm almost certain—had done him a tremendous favor once, possibly without realizing how valuable it truly was, and he wished he had a fortune because he would leave it to you when he died, along with a curse for each of the other citizens. Now then, if you were the one who did him that favor, you are his rightful heir and entitled to the bag of gold. I know I can rely on your honor and integrity, because in a citizen of Hadleyburg these qualities are a guaranteed inheritance, so I'm going to share with you what he said, completely confident that if you're not the right person, you'll search for and find the right one and make sure that poor Goodson's debt of gratitude for the service in question gets repaid. This is what he said: 'you Are Far From Being A Bad Man: Go, And Reform.'"

"HOWARD L. STEPHENSON."

"Oh, Edward, the money belongs to us, and I'm so thankful, oh, so thankful—kiss me, darling, it's been forever since we kissed—and we needed it so desperately—the money—and now you're free from Pinkerton and his bank, and you're nobody's slave anymore; I feel like I could soar with happiness."

It was a blissful thirty minutes that the husband and wife spent together on the sofa, tenderly embracing one another; it felt like the good old times had returned—those days that had started during their courtship and continued uninterrupted until the outsider arrived with that cursed money. After a while, the wife spoke:

"Oh, Edward, how fortunate it was that you did that wonderful favor for him, poor Goodson! I never cared for him before, but I love him now. And it was noble and beautiful of you to never mention it or boast about it." Then, with a hint of reproach, "But you should have told me, Edward, you should have told your wife, you know."

"Well, I—uh—well, Mary, you see—"

"Stop beating around the bush and tell me what happened, Edward. I've always loved you, and now I'm proud of you. Everyone believed there was only one good, generous person in this village, but now it's clear that you—Edward, why won't you tell me?"

"Well—uh—uh—Why, Mary, I can't!"

"You can't? Why can't you?"

"You see, he—well, he—he made me promise I wouldn't."

The wife looked him over and said very slowly:

"Made—you—promise? Edward, why are you telling me this?"

"Mary, do you think I would lie?"

She felt troubled and remained quiet for a moment, then she placed her hand in his and said:

"No... no. We've strayed too far from what we know to be true—may God protect us from that! Throughout your entire life, you've never told a lie. But now—now that everything we've built our lives on seems to be falling apart beneath us, we—we—" Her voice failed her for a moment, then she said, her words breaking, "Lead us not into temptation... I believe you made that promise, Edward. Let's leave it at that. Let's stay away from that dangerous territory. Now—all of that is behind us; let's be happy once more; this isn't the time for dark thoughts."

Edward found it somewhat difficult to follow along, as his thoughts kept drifting away—attempting to recall what favor he had done for Goodson.

The couple stayed awake most of the night, Mary feeling happy and occupied with her thoughts, while Edward was preoccupied but far from content. Mary was making plans for how she would spend the money. Edward was attempting to remember that favor he had done.

Initially his conscience troubled him because of the lie he had told Mary—if it actually was a lie. After considerable thought—what if it was a lie? So what? Was it really such a significant thing? Don't we constantly live lies through our actions? Then why shouldn't we speak them as well? Look at Mary—consider what she had done. While he was rushing off to do the right thing, what had she been doing? Regretting that the papers hadn't been destroyed and the money kept for themselves. Is stealing worse than lying?

That concern lost its bite—the lie faded into the background and left a sense of relief in its place. The next issue came forward: had he actually provided that service? Well, here was Goodson's own testimony as described in Stephenson's letter; there couldn't be better evidence than that—it even proved that he had provided it. Naturally. So that matter was resolved. . . No, not entirely. He remembered with a cringe that this unknown Mr. Stephenson was just slightly uncertain about whether the person who performed it was Richards or someone else—and, oh no, he had placed Richards on his honor! He had to decide for himself where that money should go—and Mr. Stephenson wasn't questioning that if he was the wrong person he would act honorably and locate the right one. Oh, it was terrible to place a man in such a position—ah, why couldn't Stephenson have omitted that uncertainty? What made him want to include that?

Further thought. How did Richards's name stay in Stephenson's memory as the right person, rather than someone else's name? That seemed promising. Yes, that appeared very promising indeed. Actually, it kept looking more and more convincing as time went on—until eventually it became absolute proof. Then Richards immediately dismissed the matter from his thoughts, because he had a personal intuition that once proof is established, it's better to leave it alone.

He was feeling reasonably comfortable now, but there was still one other detail that kept pushing itself on his notice: of course he had done that service—that was settled; but what was that service? He must recall it—he would not go to sleep till he had recalled it; it would make his peace of mind perfect. And so he thought and thought. He thought of a dozen things—possible services, even probable services—but none of them seemed adequate, none of them seemed large enough, none of them seemed worth the money—worth the fortune Goodson had wished he could leave in his will. And besides, he couldn't remember having done them, anyway. Now, then—now, then—what kind of a service would it be that would make a man so incredibly grateful? Ah—the saving of his soul! That must be it. Yes, he could remember, now, how he once set himself the task of converting Goodson, and worked at it as much as—he was going to say three months; but upon closer examination it shrank to a month, then to a week, then to a day, then to nothing. Yes, he remembered now, and with unwelcome clarity, that Goodson had told him to go to hell and mind his own business—he wasn't eager to follow Hadleyburg to heaven!

So that solution was a failure—he hadn't saved Goodson's soul. Richards felt discouraged. Then after a moment came another idea: had he saved Goodson's property? No, that wouldn't work—he didn't have any. His life? That was it! Of course. Why hadn't he thought of it before? This time he was on the right track, for sure. His imagination was working hard now, spinning away.

For the next two grueling hours, he found himself desperately trying to figure out how he had saved

Goodson's life. He imagined rescuing him in countless dangerous and challenging situations. Each time, he managed to work out the details perfectly up to a certain point; then, just when he was starting to convince himself that it had actually happened, some problematic detail would emerge that made the entire scenario impossible. Take the drowning incident, for example. In that version, he had swum out and dragged an unconscious Goodson back to shore while a large crowd watched and cheered, but once he had worked through all the details and was beginning to recall everything clearly, a flood of contradictory facts came rushing in: the whole town would have heard about such an event, Mary certainly would have known about it, and it would shine like a spotlight in his memory rather than being some modest good deed he might have done "without knowing its full value." And then he remembered that he couldn't even swim.

Ah—there was a point he had been overlooking from the beginning: it had to be a service he had provided "possibly without knowing the full value of it." Well, really, that should be an easy search—much easier than those other ones. And sure enough, eventually he found it. Goodson, years and years ago, came close to marrying a very sweet and pretty girl named Nancy Hewitt, but somehow the engagement had been called off; the girl died, Goodson remained unmarried, and eventually became bitter and openly contemptuous of humanity. Shortly after the girl's death, the town discovered, or believed it had discovered, that she had a trace of Black ancestry in her bloodline. Richards pondered these details for quite a while, and finally he thought he recalled things about them that must have been forgotten in his memory due to years of neglect. He seemed to vaguely remember that he was the one who discovered the Black ancestry; that he was the one who told the town; that the town told Goodson where they learned it; that he thereby saved Goodson from marrying the girl with mixed heritage; that he had performed this great service "without knowing the full value of it," actually without realizing he was doing it; but that Goodson understood its value, and what a close call he had experienced, and so went to his grave thankful to his benefactor and wishing he had a fortune to leave him. Everything was clear and simple now, and the more he reviewed it, the brighter and more certain it became; and finally, when he settled down to sleep, content and happy, he remembered the entire incident as if it had happened yesterday. In fact, he vaguely recalled Goodson expressing his gratitude to him once. Meanwhile, Mary had spent six thousand dollars on a new house for herself and a pair of slippers for her pastor, and then had drifted peacefully off to sleep.

That same Saturday evening, the mail carrier had brought a letter to each of the other leading citizens—nineteen letters altogether. None of the envelopes looked the same, and each address was written in different handwriting, but the letters inside were identical to one another in every way except for one detail. They were perfect duplicates of the letter that Richards had received—including the handwriting—and all bore Stephenson's signature, but instead of Richards's name, each letter contained the recipient's own name.

All night long, eighteen leading citizens did exactly what their fellow townsman Richards was doing at that very moment—they devoted all their energy to trying to recall what remarkable service they had unknowingly performed for Barclay Goodson. In every case, it was no easy task; nevertheless, they managed to succeed.

While they struggled with this difficult task, their wives spent the night doing something much easier—spending the money. In just one night, the nineteen wives managed to spend an average of seven thousand dollars each from the forty thousand in the sack, totaling one hundred and thirty-three thousand dollars altogether.

The next day brought a surprise for Jack Halliday. He observed that the faces of the nineteen leading citizens and their wives displayed that same expression of serene and sacred joy once more. He couldn't comprehend it, nor could he come up with any comments that might harm or upset it. Consequently, it became his turn to feel discontented with life. His personal theories about the reasons behind their happiness proved wrong in every case when he investigated them. When he encountered Mrs. Wilcox and saw the calm bliss on her face, he thought to himself, "Her cat must have had kittens"—so he went and questioned the cook; this wasn't the case, though the cook had also noticed the happiness but didn't know what caused it. When Halliday discovered the same bliss on the face of "Shadbelly" Billson (his village nickname), he felt certain that one of Billson's neighbors had broken a leg, but his inquiries revealed this hadn't occurred. The quiet joy on Gregory Yates's face could only mean one thing—he must be rid of his mother-in-law; this was yet another wrong guess. "And Pinkerton—Pinkerton—he must have collected ten cents that he expected to lose." And it continued like this, one guess after another. In some situations his theories had to remain uncertain, while in others they turned out to be clear mistakes. Eventually Halliday told himself, "At least it confirms that nineteen Hadleyburg families are temporarily experiencing heaven: I don't understand how this came about; I only know that Providence must be taking the day off."

An architect and builder from a neighboring state had recently decided to start a small business in this unpromising village, and his sign had been displayed for a week now. He hadn't attracted a single customer yet; he felt discouraged and regretted his decision to come. However, his fortune was about to change dramatically. First one and then another prominent citizen's wife approached him privately:

"Come to my house a week from Monday—but don't mention it to anyone right now. We're thinking about building."

He received eleven invitations that day. That evening he wrote to his daughter and called off her engagement to her student. He told her she could marry someone far better than that.

Pinkerton the banker and two or three other wealthy men made plans for country estates—but they held back. Those types don't count their chickens before they hatch.

The Wilsons came up with an exciting new idea—a costume party. They didn't make any firm commitments, but they quietly told everyone they knew that they were considering it and thought they might host one—"and if we do, you'll definitely be invited, of course." People were shocked and whispered to each other, "What are they thinking? Those poor Wilsons can't possibly afford something like that." Several of the nineteen women spoke privately to their husbands, saying, "It's actually a good idea. We'll stay quiet until their shabby little party is finished, then we'll throw one that will completely overshadow theirs."

The days passed by, and the list of planned future spending grew higher and higher, wilder and wilder, more and more foolish and reckless. It started to appear as though every member of the nineteen would not only spend his entire forty thousand dollars before the day he received it, but would actually be in debt by the time he got the money. In some cases, impulsive people didn't stop at just planning to spend—they actually spent money on credit. They purchased land, mortgages, farms, speculative stocks, fine clothes, horses, and various other things, paid the down payment, and made themselves responsible for the remainder—due in ten days. Soon, clearer thinking returned, and Halliday observed that a terrible anxiety was starting to appear on many faces. Once again he was confused and didn't know what to think of it. "The Wilcox kittens aren't dead, since they weren't born; nobody's broken a leg; there's no decrease in mother-in-laws; nothing has happened—it is an unsolvable mystery."

There was another confused man as well—Reverend Mr. Burgess. For days, wherever he went, people seemed to trail him or watch for him; and whenever he found himself in a secluded place, one of the nineteen would inevitably appear, secretly slip an envelope into his hand, whisper "To be opened at the town hall Friday evening," then disappear like someone with a guilty conscience. He had anticipated that there might be one person claiming the sack—though he had doubts, since Goodson was dead—but it never crossed his mind that this entire group might all be claimants. When the momentous Friday finally arrived, he discovered that he had nineteen envelopes.

———————

Chapter III.

The town hall had never appeared more magnificent. The platform at the far end was decorated with an impressive display of draped flags; festoons of flags hung at regular intervals along the walls; the gallery fronts were adorned with flags; the supporting columns were wrapped in flags; all of this was designed to make an impression on the visitors, since they would be attending in large numbers, and many of them would be connected to the press. The building was packed. All 412 permanent seats were taken; the 68 additional chairs that had been squeezed into the aisles were also occupied; people sat on the platform steps; some notable visitors were provided with seats on the platform itself; at the horseshoe arrangement of tables that bordered the front and sides of the platform sat a substantial group of special correspondents who had traveled from all over. It was the most elegantly dressed audience the town had ever assembled. There were some quite expensive outfits present, and in several instances the women wearing them appeared uncomfortable with such formal attire. At least that's what the townspeople thought they observed, though this impression might have stemmed from the town's awareness that these women had never worn such elaborate clothing before.

The gold sack sat on a small table at the front of the stage where everyone in the audience could see it clearly. Most of the crowd stared at it with intense fascination, their mouths practically watering with desire, their expressions filled with longing and pitiful yearning. A small group of nineteen couples looked at it with tender affection, loving gazes, and a sense of ownership, while the men in this group kept rehearsing in their minds the heartfelt spontaneous speeches of gratitude they planned to stand up and deliver soon, thanking the audience for their applause and congratulations. Occasionally, one of these men would pull a piece of paper from his vest pocket and steal a quick glance at it to jog his memory.

Of course there was a buzz of conversation happening—there always is; but finally, when Reverend Mr. Burgess stood up and placed his hand on the sack, the place became so quiet he could hear his microbes gnaw. He told the strange story of the sack, then continued to speak warmly about Hadleyburg's long-standing and well-deserved reputation for perfect honesty, and the town's justified pride in this reputation. He said this reputation was a treasure of immeasurable worth; that under Providence its value had now become incredibly enhanced, because the recent incident had spread this fame far and wide, and had therefore focused the attention of the American world upon this village, making its name forever, as he hoped and believed, synonymous with commercial integrity. [Applause.] "And who will be the guardian of this noble reputation— the community as a whole? No! The responsibility belongs to individuals, not the community. From this day forward each and every one of you is personally its special guardian, and individually responsible to ensure no harm comes to it. Do you—does each of you—accept this great trust? [Tumultuous assent.] Then all is well. Pass it on to your children and to your children's children. Today your purity is beyond question—make sure it stays that way. Today there isn't a person in your community who could be tempted to touch a penny that isn't theirs—make sure you remain in this state of grace. ["We will! we will!"] This isn't the place to make comparisons between ourselves and other communities—some of them unfriendly toward us; they have their ways, we have ours; let us be satisfied. [Applause.] I am finished. Under my hand, my friends, lies a stranger's eloquent recognition of what we are; through him the world will always know from now on what we are. We don't know who he is, but in your name I express your gratitude, and ask you to raise your voices in agreement."

The entire house rose to its feet as one and made the walls shake with thunderous applause that lasted for a full minute. Then everyone sat back down, and Mr. Burgess pulled an envelope from his pocket. The house fell completely silent as he carefully opened the envelope and removed a slip of paper from inside. He read what was written on it slowly and with great emphasis, while the audience listened in mesmerized silence to this magical document, where every single word represented a bar of gold:

""The comment I made to the troubled stranger was this: "You are far from being a bad person; go, and change your ways.""" Then he went on: "We'll find out right now whether the comment quoted here matches the one hidden in the bag; and if it turns out to be the same—which it certainly will—this bag of gold belongs to a fellow citizen who will from now on stand before the nation as the symbol of the special virtue that has made our town famous throughout the land—Mr. Billson!"

The house had prepared itself to erupt into the appropriate storm of applause, but instead of doing so, it appeared struck by paralysis. A profound silence lasted for a moment or two, then a wave of whispered murmurs swept through the place with roughly this meaning: "Billson! Oh, come on, this is ridiculous! Twenty dollars to a stranger—or anyone—Billson! Tell it to someone who'll believe it!" At this moment the house suddenly caught its breath in a fresh surge of amazement, because it realized that while Deacon Billson stood in one section of the hall with his head humbly lowered, Lawyer Wilson was doing exactly the same thing in another section. A bewildered silence followed for some time. Everyone felt confused, and nineteen couples were both surprised and outraged.

Billson and Wilson turned and stared at each other. Billson asked sharply:

"Why are you getting up, Mr. Wilson?"

"Because I have the right to. Perhaps you would be kind enough to explain to the house why you are standing up."

"With great pleasure. Because I wrote that paper."

"That's a bold-faced lie! I wrote it myself."

Burgess was now the one frozen in place. He stood there staring blankly at one man, then the other, appearing completely lost about what he should do. The entire house sat in stunned silence. At this moment, Lawyer Wilson stepped forward and spoke:

"I ask the Chair to read the name signed to that paper."

That snapped the Chair back to attention, and it announced the name:

"John Wharton Billson."

"There!" Billson shouted. "What do you have to say for yourself now? And what kind of apology are you going to give me and this insulted house for the deception you've tried to pull off here?"

"You don't owe me any apologies, sir; and regarding everything else, I'm publicly accusing you of stealing my note from Mr. Burgess and replacing it with a copy that bears your signature. There's no other possible way you could have obtained that test phrase; I'm the only person alive who knew the exact wording of that secret."

There would probably be a shocking situation if this continued; everyone observed with concern that the stenographers were writing frantically; many people were shouting "Chair, chair! Order! order!" Burgess struck with his gavel, and said:

"Let's not forget what's proper here. There's clearly been some kind of mistake, but that's surely all it is. If Mr. Wilson gave me an envelope—and I do remember now that he did—I still have it."

He pulled one from his pocket, opened it, took a quick look, and appeared both surprised and troubled, standing quietly for several moments. Then he gestured with his hand in a confused and automatic manner, attempted once or twice to speak, but then gave up in despair. Multiple voices called out:

"Read it! Read it! What is it?"

So he started speaking, in a confused and dreamlike way:

"'The comment I made to that unfortunate stranger was this: "You are far from being a bad man. [The house gazed at him marvelling.] Go, and reform."' [Murmurs: "Amazing! what can this mean?"] This one," said the Chair, "is signed Thurlow G. Wilson."

"There!" Wilson shouted, "I figure that settles it! I knew perfectly well my note was stolen."

"Stolen!" Billson shot back. "I'll have you know that neither you nor any man of your sort dare to—"

The Chair: "Order, gentlemen, order! Take your seats, both of you, please."

They followed the order, shaking their heads and muttering angrily under their breath. The entire household was deeply confused; no one knew how to handle this strange situation. After a moment, Thompson stood up. Thompson worked as a hat maker. He would have loved to

42

be one of the Nineteeners, but that wasn't meant for him; his hat inventory wasn't substantial enough to qualify for such a position. He spoke:

"Mr. Chairman, if I may be allowed to make a suggestion, is it possible that both of these gentlemen are telling the truth? I'm asking you, sir, could both of them have actually said the exact same words to the stranger? It appears to me—"

The tanner stood up and cut him off. The tanner was a bitter man who felt he deserved to be one of the Nineteeners, but he couldn't gain acceptance. This made him somewhat disagreeable in his behavior and the way he spoke. He said:

"Look, that's not the point! That could happen—twice in a hundred years—but not the other thing. Neither of them gave the twenty dollars!" [A ripple of applause.]

Billson. "I did!"

Wilson. "I did!"

Then each one accused the other of stealing.

The Chair. "Order! Sit down, if you please—both of you. Neither of the notes has been out of my possession at any moment."

A Voice. "Good—that settles that!"

The Tanner. "Mr. Chairman, one thing is clear now: one of these men has been listening in under the other man's bed and stealing family secrets. If it's not against parliamentary rules to say so, I'll point out that both of them are capable of such behavior. [The Chair. "Order! order!"] I take back that comment, sir, and I'll limit myself to suggesting that if one of them overheard the other tell his wife the test phrase, we'll catch him right now."

A Voice. "How?"

The Tanner. "Easily. The two haven't quoted the comment using exactly the same words. You would have noticed that if there hadn't been a significant amount of time and an intense argument placed between the two readings."

A Voice. "Name the difference."

The Tanner. "The word very appears in Billson's note, but not in the other."

Many Voices. "That's exactly right—he's absolutely correct!"

The Tanner. "And so, if the Chair will examine the test-remark in the sack, we shall know which of these two frauds—[The Chair. "Order!"]—which of these two adventurers—[The Chair. "Order! order!"]—which of these two gentlemen—[laughter and applause]—is entitled to wear the belt as being the first dishonest blatherskite ever bred in this town—which he has dishonored, and which will be a sultry place for him from now out!" [Vigorous applause.]

Many Voices. "Open it!—open the sack!"

Mr. Burgess cut open the sack, slipped his hand inside, and pulled out an envelope. Inside were a few folded pieces of paper. He said:

"One of these is marked, 'Not to be examined until all written communications which have been addressed to the Chair—if any—shall have been read.' The other is marked 'The Test.' Allow me. It reads as follows:

"'I don't need the first part of what my benefactor said to me to be quoted exactly, since it wasn't particularly memorable and could easily be forgotten; but the final fifteen words are quite memorable, and I believe they're easy to remember; unless these are reproduced accurately, the person claiming this should be considered a fraud. My benefactor started by saying he rarely gave advice to anyone, but when he did offer it, it always carried the mark of great value. Then he said this—and it has never left my memory: 'You are far from being a bad man—'"

Fifty Voices. "That settles it—the money's Wilson's! Wilson! Wilson! Speech! Speech!"

People jumped to their feet and gathered around Wilson, shaking his hand and offering enthusiastic congratulations—meanwhile the Chair was pounding with the gavel and shouting:

"Order, gentlemen! Order! Order! Let me finish reading, please." When quiet was restored, the reading continued as follows:

"'Go and change your ways—or mark my words—someday, because of your sins, you will die and go to hell or Hadleyburg—TRY AND MAKE IT THE FORMER.'"

A terrible silence fell over the room. At first, an angry expression began to spread across the faces of the townspeople; then, after a moment, that anger started to fade, and a look of amusement tried to replace it; the effort to suppress their laughter was so intense that it caused them great and obvious strain; the newspaper reporters, the visitors from Brixton, and other outsiders lowered their heads and covered their faces with their hands, managing to contain themselves only through sheer willpower and polite restraint. At this worst possible moment, a single voice shattered the quiet—Jack Halliday's:

"That's got the hallmark on it!"

Then the house completely lost control, strangers and everyone else included. Even Mr. Burgess's serious composure eventually cracked, and then the audience felt they had official permission to abandon all self-control, making the most of this freedom. The laughter was long and powerfully enthusiastic, but it finally died down—just long enough for Mr. Burgess to attempt continuing and for people to partially dry their eyes; then it erupted again, and then once more after that; finally Burgess managed to speak these solemn words:

"There's no point in trying to hide the truth—we're dealing with something extremely serious. This affects your town's reputation and damages its good standing. The fact that there was only one word different between the test statements given by Mr. Wilson and Mr. Billson is deeply troubling, because it shows that one of these men must have stolen something—"

The two men sat slumped and lifeless, completely drained of energy and spirit; but when they heard these words, both were suddenly energized into action and began to rise.

"Sit down!" the Chair said sharply, and they complied. "That situation, as I mentioned, was serious. And it was— but only for one of them. However, the matter has grown more severe; the reputation of both men is now in terrible danger. Should I go further and say they're in hopeless danger? Both omitted the same critical fifteen words." He stopped speaking. For several moments he let the deep silence build and strengthen its powerful effect, then continued: "There appears to be only one way this could have happened. I ask these gentlemen—Was there conspiracy?—some kind of agreement?"

A quiet whisper spread throughout the house, carrying the message: "He's got them both."

Billson wasn't accustomed to emergencies; he sat there in a state of helpless collapse. But Wilson was a lawyer. He struggled to get to his feet, pale and worried, and said:

"I ask for the patience of everyone here while I explain this deeply troubling situation. I regret having to say what

46

I'm about to say, since it will cause permanent damage to Mr. Billson's reputation—a man I have always held in high regard and respected until this moment, and whose ability to resist temptation I completely trusted, just as all of you did. However, to protect my own honor, I must speak openly and honestly. I admit with great shame—and I now beg your forgiveness for this—that I spoke every single word contained in the test phrase to that desperate stranger, including the insulting final fifteen words. [Sensation.] When the recent announcement was made public, I remembered those words, and I decided to claim the bag of money, since I had every right to it. Now I want you to think carefully about this point and consider it thoroughly: that stranger's appreciation toward me that evening was boundless; he told me himself that he couldn't find adequate words to express it, and that if he ever had the chance, he would repay me a thousand times over. So now I ask you this: could I have expected—could I have believed—could I have even remotely imagined—that someone who felt so grateful would do something so thankless as to add those completely unnecessary fifteen words to his test? Would he set a trap for me? Would he expose me as someone who speaks badly of my own town in front of my own neighbors gathered in a public meeting hall? The idea was ridiculous; it was unthinkable. His test would only include the kind opening part of what I had said. I had absolutely no doubt about that. You would have thought the same way I did. You wouldn't have expected such a cruel betrayal from someone you had helped and against whom you had done nothing wrong. So with complete confidence and total trust, I wrote down the opening words on a piece of paper— ending with "Go, and reform"—and signed it. Just as I was about to put it in an envelope, someone called me to my back office, and without thinking, I left the paper lying open on my desk." He paused, slowly turned his head toward Billson, waited a moment, then continued: "I want you to take note of this: when I came back a short time later, Mr. Billson was leaving through my front door." [Sensation.]

In an instant, Billson jumped to his feet and began shouting:

"It's a lie! It's a disgraceful lie!"

The Chair. "Please take a seat, sir! Mr. Wilson has the floor."

Billson's friends dragged him back to his chair and calmed him down, while Wilson continued speaking:

"Those are the simple facts. My note was now lying in a different place on the table from where I had left it. I noticed this, but didn't think it was important, assuming a draft had blown it there. The idea that Mr. Billson would read a private paper never crossed my mind; he was an honorable man, and such behavior would be beneath him. If I may say so, I believe his additional word 'very' can be explained: it's due to a memory lapse. I was the only person in the world who could provide any detail about the test-mark through honorable means. I have finished."

Nothing in the world can confuse people's thinking and shake their beliefs and corrupt their feelings quite like a convincing speech, especially when the audience isn't familiar with the tricks and deceptions that speakers use. Wilson sat down in triumph. The crowd overwhelmed him with waves of enthusiastic applause; friends rushed over to shake his hand and offer their congratulations, while Billson was drowned out by shouting and couldn't get a word in. The Chair pounded and pounded with the gavel, continuously shouting:

"But let's move forward, gentlemen, let's move forward!"

At last there was a noticeable amount of quiet, and the hatter said:

"But what is there to proceed with, sir, but to deliver the money?"

Voices. "That's it! That's it! Come forward, Wilson!"

"I propose three cheers for Mr. Wilson, who represents the special virtue that—"

The cheers erupted before he could complete his sentence, and amid the celebration—along with the loud banging of the gavel—some excited supporters lifted Wilson onto a large friend's shoulders and were about to carry him triumphantly to the platform. The Chairman's voice now rose above the commotion:

"Order! To your places! You forget that there is still a document to be read." When silence had returned, he picked up the document and was about to read it, but set it down again, saying "I forgot; this cannot be read until all written communications I have received are first read." He pulled an envelope from his pocket, took out what was inside, looked at it—appeared shocked—held it up and stared at it—gazed at it intently.

Twenty or thirty voices shouted out

"What is it? Read it! read it!"

And he did—slowly, and with wonder:

"'The comment I made to the stranger—[Voices. "Hello! how's this?"]—was this: 'You are far from being a bad man. [Voices. "Great Scott!"] Go, and reform.'" [Voice. "Oh, saw my leg off!"] Signed by Mr. Pinkerton the banker."

The explosion of joy that erupted was the kind that would make any reasonable person cry. Those who weren't affected laughed until tears streamed down their faces; the reporters, overcome with laughter, scribbled illegible marks that could never be read; and a sleeping dog leaped up in terror and barked frantically at the chaos. All kinds of shouts rang out through the noise: "We're getting rich—two Symbols of Incorruptibility!—not even counting Billson!" "Three!—include Shadbelly too—we can't have too many!" "That's right—Billson's elected!" "Poor Wilson! victim of two thieves!"

A Powerful Voice. "Quiet! The Chair has pulled something else from its pocket."

Voices. "Hooray! Is this something new? Read it! Read! Read!"

The Chair [reading]. "'The remark which I made,' and so on. 'You are far from being a bad man. Go,' and so forth. Signed, 'Gregory Yates.'"

Tornado of Voices. "Four Symbols!" "Hooray for Yates!" "Fish again!"

The house was now in an uproarious mood, eager to squeeze every bit of entertainment from the situation. Several members of the Committee of Nineteen, looking pale and troubled, stood up and started making their way toward the aisles, but dozens of voices shouted out:

"The doors, the doors—close the doors; no Incorruptible shall leave this place! Sit down, everybody!" The order was followed.

"Fish again! Read! read!"

The Chair tried again, and once more the same familiar words started flowing from its lips—"'You are far from being a bad man—'"

"Name! name! What's his name?"

"'L. Ingoldsby Sargent.'"

"Five elected! Pile up the Symbols! Go on, go on!"

"'You are far from being a bad—'"

"Name! name!"

"'Nicholas Whitworth.'"

"Hooray! hooray! it's a symbolical day!"

Someone burst in and started singing this verse (omitting "it's") to the beautiful "Mikado" melody of "When a man's afraid of a beautiful maid;" the audience enthusiastically joined along; then, at just the right moment, someone else added another line—

"And don't forget this—"

The house thundered with the sound. A third line was immediately provided—

"Corruptibles far from Hadleyburg are—"

The house erupted in applause for that one as well. As the final note faded away, Jack Halliday's voice soared high and clear, carrying with it a closing line—

"But the Symbols are here, you bet!"

That was sung with thunderous enthusiasm. Then the joyful crowd started from the beginning and sang all four lines twice, with tremendous energy and spirit, and concluded with a resounding three cheers and a tiger for "Hadleyburg the Incorruptible and all Symbols of it which we shall find worthy to receive the hall-mark tonight."

Then the shouting at the Chair started up again, everywhere:

"Keep going! Keep going! Read! Read more! Read everything you have!"

"That's it—keep going! We are achieving eternal fame!"

A dozen men stood up and started protesting. They declared that this ridiculous charade was the work of some reckless prankster, and it was an insult to the entire community. Without question, these signatures were all fake—

"Sit down! Sit down! Shut up! You are confessing. We'll find your names in the group."

"Mr. Chairman, how many of those envelopes do you have?"

The Chair counted.

"Including the ones we've already looked at, there are nineteen."

A wave of mocking applause erupted.

"Maybe they all hold the secret. I suggest that you open every one of them and read each signature that's attached to that type of note—and also read the first eight words of each note."

"I second the motion!"

It was proposed and approved—with thunderous enthusiasm. Then poor old Richards stood up, and his wife rose to stand beside him. She kept her head lowered so no one could see her tears. Her husband offered her his arm for support, and with her leaning on him, he started to speak in a trembling voice:

"My friends, you have known both of us—Mary and me—our entire lives, and I believe you have cared for us and held us in high regard—"

The Chair interrupted him:

"Let me speak. What you're saying is absolutely true, Mr. Richards; this town really does know you both; it genuinely likes you; it truly respects you; more than that—it honors you and loves you—"

Halliday's voice rang out:

"That's the absolute truth! If the Chairman is correct, let everyone in the house speak up and confirm it. Stand up! Now then—hip! hip! hip!—all together!"

The entire audience stood up together, turned eagerly toward the elderly couple, filled the air with a flurry of waving handkerchiefs, and delivered their cheers with all the warmth and affection in their hearts.

The Chair then continued:

"What I was going to say is this: We know you have a good heart, Mr. Richards, but this isn't the time to show charity toward wrongdoers. [Shouts of "Right! right!"] I can see your generous intentions written on your face, but I can't let you speak up for these men—"

"But I was going to—"

"Please take your seat, Mr. Richards. We need to review the remaining notes—basic fairness to the men who have already been revealed demands this. As soon as we've finished that—I give you my word—you will be heard."

Many voices called out. "Right!—the Chair is correct—no interruption can be allowed at this point! Continue!—the names! the names!—according to the terms of the motion!"

The elderly couple reluctantly took their seats, and the husband whispered to his wife, "It's painfully difficult to have to wait; the embarrassment will be even worse when they discover we were only coming to ask for help for ourselves."

Immediately the cheerful excitement erupted once more as the names were read aloud.

"'You are far from being a bad man—' Signed, 'Robert J. Titmarsh.'"

"'You are far from being a bad man—' Signed, 'Eliphalet Weeks.'"

"'You are far from being a bad man—' Signature, 'Oscar B. Wilder.'"

At this point the crowd decided to take the eight words away from the Chairman's control. He was grateful for this relief. From then on, he simply held up each note one by one and waited. The assembly chanted the eight words together in a deep, rhythmic, musical chorus (which sounded remarkably similar to a familiar church hymn)— "You are f-a-r from being a b-a-a-a-d man." Then the Chairman announced, "Signature, 'Archibald Wilcox.'" And it continued this way, name after name, with everyone having an increasingly wonderful time except the miserable Nineteen. Occasionally, when an especially prominent name was announced, the crowd made the Chairman pause while they chanted the entire test phrase from start to finish, "And go to hell or Hadleyburg—try and make it the for-or-m-e-r!" and during these special moments they added a grand, tortured, and dramatic "A-a-a-a-men!"

The list grew shorter and shorter and shorter, with poor old Richards keeping track of the count, flinching whenever a name that sounded like his own was called out, and waiting in wretched anxiety for the moment when it would be his humiliating duty to stand up with Mary and deliver his plea, which he planned to phrase like this: "... for until now we have never done anything wrong, but have lived our simple lives without reproach. We are very poor, we are old, and have no children to help us; we were severely tempted, and we gave in. It was my intention when I stood up earlier to confess and ask that my name not be announced in this public place, for it seemed to us that we could not endure it; but I was stopped. It was right; it was our responsibility to suffer along with the others. It has been difficult for us. This is the first time we have ever heard our name spoken by anyone—tainted. Be kind—for the sake of better times; make our disgrace as easy to bear as your compassion allows." At this moment in his daydream Mary elbowed him, noticing that his attention had wandered. The crowd was chanting, "You are f-a-r," etc.

"Get ready," Mary whispered. "Your name is coming up next; he's already called eighteen names."

The chant ended.

"Next! Next! Next!" echoed throughout the entire house from every direction.

Burgess reached into his pocket. The elderly couple, shaking, started to stand up. Burgess searched around for a moment, then spoke:

"I find I have read them all."

Overwhelmed with joy and amazement, the couple collapsed into their chairs, and Mary whispered:

"Oh, thank God, we're saved!—he's lost ours—I wouldn't trade this for a hundred of those sacks!"

The house erupted with its "Mikado" parody, and performed it three times with growing excitement, standing up when they reached the final line for the third time—

"But the Symbols are here, you bet!"

and wrapping up with cheers and a rousing cheer for "Hadleyburg's moral integrity and our eighteen eternal symbols of it."

Then Wingate, the saddler, stood up and suggested they give cheers "for the cleanest man in town, the one solitary important citizen in it who didn't try to steal that money— Edward Richards."

They were offered with tremendous and touching sincerity; then someone suggested that "Richards should be chosen as the sole Guardian and Symbol of the now Sacred Hadleyburg Tradition, with the authority and right to stand up and face the entire sarcastic world."

Approved by unanimous acclaim; then they performed the "Mikado" once more, and concluded with—

"And there's one Symbol left, you bet!"

There was a pause; then—

A Voice. "Alright then, who's going to get fired?"

The Tanner spoke with bitter sarcasm. "That's simple enough. The money needs to be split among the eighteen Incorruptibles. They each gave the suffering stranger twenty dollars—along with that comment—each taking their turn—it took twenty-two minutes for the entire procession to pass by. They staked the stranger—total contributions came to $360. All they're asking for now is just their loan returned—plus interest—forty thousand dollars in total."

Many Voices [mockingly.] "That's it! Share it! Share it! Be generous to the poor—don't make them wait!"

The Chair. "Order! I now present the stranger's remaining document. It reads: 'If no one comes forward to claim this [loud chorus of groans], I wish for you to open the bag and distribute the money to the leading citizens of your town, who should hold it in trust [Cries of "Oh! Oh! Oh!"], and use it in whatever ways they believe will best promote and maintain your community's distinguished reputation for unwavering honesty [more cries]—a reputation that their names and their efforts will enhance with new and widespread honor." [Enthusiastic burst of mocking applause.] That appears to be everything. No—there's a postscript here:

"'P.S.—CITIZENS OF HADLEYBURG: There is no test-remark—nobody made one. [Great sensation.] There wasn't any poor stranger, nor any twenty-dollar contribution, nor any accompanying blessing and compliment—these are all made-up stories. [General buzz and hum of astonishment and delight.] Let me tell you my story—it will only take a word or two. I passed through your town at a certain time, and received a deep insult which I had not deserved. Any other man would have been satisfied to kill one or two of you and call it even, but to me that would have been a small

56

revenge, and not enough; for the dead do not suffer. Besides I could not kill you all—and, anyway, made as I am, even that would not have satisfied me. I wanted to harm every man in the place, and every woman—and not in their bodies or in their property, but in their pride—the place where weak and foolish people are most defenseless. So I disguised myself and came back and studied you. You were easy targets. You had an old and noble reputation for honesty, and naturally you were proud of it—it was your greatest treasure, the very apple of your eye. As soon as I discovered that you carefully and watchfully kept yourselves and your children away from temptation, I knew how to proceed. Why, you simple creatures, the weakest of all weak things is a virtue which has not been tested in the fire. I laid a plan, and gathered a list of names. My project was to corrupt Hadleyburg the Incorruptible. My idea was to make liars and thieves of nearly half a hundred spotless men and women who had never in their lives told a lie or stolen a penny. I was afraid of Goodson. He was neither born nor raised in Hadleyburg. I was afraid that if I started to operate my scheme by getting my letter laid before you, you would say to yourselves, 'Goodson is the only man among us who would give away twenty dollars to a poor devil'—and then you might not bite at my bait. But heaven took Goodson; then I knew I was safe, and I set my trap and baited it. It may be that I shall not catch all the men to whom I mailed the fake test-secret, but I shall catch most of them, if I know Hadleyburg nature. [Voices. "Right—he got every last one of them."] I believe they will even steal apparent gambling-money, rather than miss out, poor, tempted, and misguided fellows. I am hoping to eternally and everlastingly crush your vanity and give Hadleyburg a new reputation—one that will stick—and spread far. If I have succeeded, open the sack and summon the Committee on Propagation and Preservation of the Hadleyburg Reputation.'"

A Storm of Voices. "Open it! Open it! The Eighteen to the front! Committee on Propagation of the Tradition! Forward—the Incorruptibles!"

The Chair tore open the sack completely and scooped up a handful of gleaming, wide, golden coins, rattled them together, and then inspected them closely.

"Friends, they are nothing but lead discs covered in gold!"

There was a thunderous burst of joy over this news, and when the commotion had died down, the tanner shouted:

"Based on his clear seniority in this field, Mr. Wilson serves as Chairman of the Committee on Propagation of the Tradition. I recommend that he come forward to represent his colleagues and accept responsibility for the money."

A Hundred Voices. "Wilson! Wilson! Wilson! Speech! Speech!"

Wilson spoke with a voice trembling with anger. "You will allow me to say, and without apologies for my language, damn the money!"

A Voice. "Oh, and him a Baptist!"

A Voice. "Seventeen Symbols remaining! Come forward, gentlemen, and take on your responsibility!"

There was a pause—no response.

The Saddler spoke up. "Mr. Chairman, we still have one honest man remaining from our former elite, and he needs money and has earned it. I propose that you assign Jack Halliday to go up there and auction off that bag of gold twenty-dollar coins, and give the proceeds to the rightful man—the man whom Hadleyburg takes pride in honoring—Edward Richards."

58

The crowd received this with tremendous excitement, and once again the dog joined in the commotion. The saddler opened the bidding at one dollar, while the people from Brixton and Barnum's agent battled fiercely for the item. The crowd cheered with each increase in the bids, and the excitement grew higher and higher with every passing moment. The bidders became more competitive and increasingly bold, showing greater and greater determination. The bidding jumps rose from one dollar to five, then climbed to ten, then leaped to twenty, then surged to fifty, then soared to one hundred, then—

At the start of the auction, Richards whispered anxiously to his wife: "Oh, Mary, can we let this happen? It—it—you see, it represents honor—a reward, recognition of moral character, and—and—can we let this continue? Shouldn't I stand up and—Oh, Mary, what should we do?— what do you think we—" [Halliday's voice rang out: "Fifteen I have!—fifteen for the sack!—twenty!—ah, thank you!— thirty—thank you again! Thirty, thirty, thirty!—do I hear forty?—forty it is! Keep the momentum going, gentlemen, keep it going!—fifty!—thank you, noble Roman!—going at fifty, fifty, fifty!—seventy!—ninety!—excellent!—one hundred!—pile it up, pile it up!—one hundred and twenty—forty!—just in time!—one hundred and fifty!— Two hundred!—superb! Do I hear two h—thank you!— two hundred and fifty!—"]

"It's another temptation, Edward—I'm trembling all over—but we've already escaped one temptation, and that should warn us to—["Did I hear six?—thank you!—six fifty, six f—SEVEN hundred!"] Still, Edward, when you consider—nobody suspects—["Eight hundred dollars!— hurrah!—make it nine!—Mr. Parsons, did I hear you say— thank you!—nine!—this magnificent sack of pure lead selling for only nine hundred dollars, gilding included—come now! do I hear—a thousand!—much appreciated!—did someone say eleven?—a sack that's going to be the most famous in the entire Uni—"] "Oh, Edward" (starting to cry), "we're so poor!—but—but—do whatever you think is right—do whatever you think is right."

Edward fell—that is, he remained seated; he sat with a conscience that wasn't at peace, but which was overwhelmed by the circumstances around him.

Meanwhile, a stranger who resembled an amateur detective dressed up as an unlikely English earl had been observing the evening's events with obvious interest and a satisfied look on his face, quietly making observations to himself. He was now thinking to himself something like this: "None of the Eighteen are placing bids; that won't do; I need to change that—the dramatic structure demands it; they must purchase the sack they attempted to steal; they must pay a steep price as well—some of them have money. And there's something else: when I make an error in Hadleyburg's nature, the man who exposes that mistake deserves a substantial reward, and someone has to pay for it. This poor old Richards has made my judgment look foolish; he is an honest man—I don't comprehend it, but I accept it. Yes, he caught my bluff—and with a straight flush, and by all rights the winnings belong to him. And it's going to be a big jackpot too, if I can arrange it. He let me down, but I'll let that slide."

He was watching the bidding. At a thousand dollars, the market collapsed: prices dropped rapidly. He waited—and continued watching. One competitor withdrew; then another, and another. He placed a bid or two at this point. When the bids had fallen to ten dollars, he added five; someone raised him three; he paused for a moment, then threw in a fifty-dollar jump, and the sack was his—at $1,282. The crowd erupted in cheers—then fell silent; for he was standing up, and had raised his hand. He began to speak.

"I want to say something and ask for a favor. I'm a dealer in rare items, and I do business with people interested in coin collecting all around the world. I can make a profit on this purchase just as it is; but there's a way, if I can get your approval, that I can make every one of these lead twenty-dollar pieces worth its face value in gold, and maybe even more. Give me that approval, and I'll share part of my profits with your Mr. Richards, whose unshakeable honesty you have so rightfully and warmly recognized tonight; his portion will be ten thousand dollars, and I'll give him the money tomorrow. [Loud applause from the crowd. But the phrase "unshakeable honesty" made the Richardses blush charmingly; however, it was taken as modesty, and caused no trouble.] If you'll approve my proposal by a strong majority—I'd like a two-thirds vote—I'll consider that the town's agreement, and that's all I'm asking for. Rare items are always enhanced by any method that will spark curiosity and force people to talk about them. Now if I may have your permission to stamp on the faces of each of these supposed coins the names of the eighteen gentlemen who"

Nine-tenths of the audience jumped to their feet instantly—dog included—and the proposal was approved with a storm of enthusiastic applause and laughter.

They sat down, and all the Symbols except "Dr." Clay Harkness stood up, angrily protesting against the suggested outrage, and threatening to—

"Please don't threaten me," the stranger said calmly. "I understand my legal rights, and I'm not used to being intimidated by empty threats." [Applause.] He took a seat. "Dr." Harkness spotted an opportunity. He was one of the

61

two wealthiest men in town, with Pinkerton being the other. Harkness owned a mint—that is, he manufactured a popular patent medicine. He was campaigning for the Legislature on one political ticket, while Pinkerton ran on the opposing one. The race was tight and heated, growing more intense each day. Both men had strong desires for wealth; each had purchased large parcels of land with specific intentions; a new railroad was coming, and both wanted to serve in the Legislature to help direct the route to benefit their own interests; a single vote could determine the outcome, along with two or three fortunes. The stakes were enormous, and Harkness was a bold risk-taker. He was seated near the stranger. While one of the other Symbols was keeping the audience occupied with objections and pleas, he leaned closer and whispered,

"What is your price for the sack?"

"Forty thousand dollars."

"I'll give you twenty."

"No."

"Twenty-five."

"No."

"Say thirty."

"The price is forty thousand dollars; not a penny less."

"All right, I'll give it to you. I will come to the hotel at ten in the morning. I don't want anyone to know about this; I'll see you privately."

"Very good." Then the stranger stood up and addressed the house:

"I realize it's getting late. These gentlemen's speeches have merit, interest, and grace, but if you'll excuse me, I need to leave now. Thank you for the great favor you've shown me by granting my request. I ask the Chair to hold onto the sack for me until tomorrow and to give these three five-hundred-dollar bills to Mr. Richards." The bills were handed up to the Chair.

"At nine o'clock I'll come for the bag, and at eleven I'll personally deliver the remaining ten thousand dollars to Mr. Richards at his house. Good night."

Then he slipped out, leaving the audience making an enormous noise that was a mixture of cheers, the "Mikado" song, dog-disapproval, and the chant, "You are f-a-r from being a b-a-a-d man—a-a-a a-men!"

IV.

At home, the Richards family had to put up with congratulations and compliments until midnight. Then they were finally alone. They appeared somewhat sad, and they sat quietly, lost in thought. Eventually Mary let out a sigh and said:

"Do you think we're at fault, Edward—really at fault?" and her gaze drifted to the condemning trio of large bills lying on the table, where the well-wishers had been admiring them and handling them with reverence. Edward didn't respond immediately; then he let out a sigh and said, hesitantly:

"We—we couldn't help it, Mary. It—well it was ordered. All things are."

Mary looked up and met his gaze steadily, but he didn't look back at her. After a moment she said:

"I used to think congratulations and praise always felt wonderful. But now it seems to me—Edward?"

"Well?"

"Are you going to stay in the bank?"

"N—no."

"Resign?"

"In the morning—by note."

"It does seem best."

Richards buried his face in his hands and whispered:

"Before, I wasn't afraid to let vast amounts of other people's money flow through my hands, but—Mary, I am so exhausted, so exhausted—"

"We will go to bed."

At nine in the morning, the stranger requested the sack and transported it to the hotel by taxi. At ten o'clock, Harkness met with him in private. The stranger requested and received five checks from a city bank—made out to "Bearer"—four checks for $1,500 each, and one for $34,000. He placed one of the smaller checks in his wallet, and the rest, totaling $38,500, he put in an envelope, along with a note he wrote after Harkness had left. At eleven o'clock, he visited the Richards' house and knocked on the door. Mrs. Richards looked through the window shutters, then went and accepted the envelope, and the stranger left without saying a word. She returned looking flushed and somewhat shaky on her feet, and breathed out:

"I'm certain I recognized him! Last night I had the feeling that perhaps I'd seen him somewhere before."

"He is the man who brought the sack here?"

"I am almost sure of it."

"Then he's also pretending to be Stephenson, and he fooled every important person in this town with his fake secret. Now if he sent checks instead of cash, we've been tricked too, just when we thought we were safe. I was starting to feel pretty good again after getting some sleep last night, but seeing that envelope makes me feel sick. It's not thick enough; $8,500 even in the biggest bills would be much bulkier than that."

"Edward, why do you have a problem with checks?"

"Checks signed by Stephenson! I'm willing to accept the $8,500 if it could come as cash—because it really does seem like that's how it was meant to be, Mary—but I've never been very brave, and I don't have the nerve to try cashing a check signed with that cursed name. It would be a trap. That man was trying to catch me; we got away somehow; and now he's attempting a different approach. If it's checks—"

"Oh, Edward, this is terrible!" And she held up the checks and began to cry.

"Throw them in the fire! Hurry! We can't let ourselves be tempted. This is a scheme to make the world mock us, just like everyone else, and—Hand them over to me, since you won't do it!" He grabbed them and attempted to maintain his hold until he could reach the stove; but he was only human, he was a cashier, and he paused for a moment to verify the signature. Then he almost fainted.

"Fan me, Mary, fan me! They are the same as gold!"

"Oh, how lovely, Edward! Why?"

"Signed by Harkness. What could the mystery behind that be, Mary?"

"Edward, do you think—"

"Look here—look at this! Fifteen—fifteen—fifteen—thirty-four. Thirty-eight thousand five hundred! Mary, the sack isn't worth twelve dollars, and Harkness—apparently—has paid about par for it."

"And do you think it all comes to us—instead of the ten thousand?"

"Well, it certainly appears that way. And the checks are made out to 'Bearer,' as well."

"Is that good, Edward? What is it for?"

"A hint to gather them at some far-off bank, I suppose. Maybe Harkness doesn't want this business to become public knowledge. What's that—a note?"

"Yes. It was with the checks."

It was written in "Stephenson's" handwriting, but there was no signature. It said:

"I am a disappointed man. Your honesty cannot be corrupted by temptation. I had a different opinion about this matter, but I was wrong about you, and I sincerely apologize. I truly respect you—and that sentiment is genuine as well. This town doesn't deserve to kiss the edge of your clothing. Dear sir, I made a firm wager with myself that there were nineteen corruptible men in your morally upright community. I was wrong. Take all the money, you've earned it."

Richards let out a deep sigh and said:

"It seems written with fire—it burns so. Mary—I am miserable again."

"I do too. Oh, sweetheart, I wish—"

"To think, Mary—he believes in me."

"Oh, don't, Edward—I can't bear it."

"If I had truly earned those beautiful words, Mary—and God knows there was a time when I believed I deserved them—I think I would gladly pay forty thousand dollars to have them back. I would treasure that paper more than gold and precious stones, and keep it with me forever. But now—we couldn't bear to live under the weight of its silent accusation, Mary."

He put it in the fire.

A messenger arrived and delivered an envelope. Richards took a note from it and read it; the message was from Burgess:

"You saved me during a difficult time. I saved you last night. It came at the cost of a lie, but I made that sacrifice willingly, and from a grateful heart. No one in this village knows as well as I do how brave and good and noble you are. Deep down you cannot respect me, knowing what you do about the matter I am accused of, and which the general opinion has condemned me for; but I ask that you will at least believe that I am a grateful man; it will help me bear my burden. [Signed] 'BURGESS.'"

"Saved, once more. And on such terms!" He threw the note into the fire. "I—I wish I were dead, Mary, I wish I could escape from all of this!"

"Oh, these are painful, painful days, Edward. The wounds, because of their very kindness, cut so deeply—and they keep coming so quickly!"

Three days before the election, each of two thousand voters suddenly discovered they owned a valuable keepsake—one of the famous fake double-eagle coins. Stamped around one side were these words: "THE REMARK I MADE TO THE POOR STRANGER WAS—" Stamped around the other side were these words: "GO, AND REFORM. [SIGNED] PINKERTON." In this way, all the remaining debris from the famous joke was dumped on a single person, with devastating results. It brought back the recent enormous laughter and focused it entirely on Pinkerton; and Harkness's election became an easy victory.

Within twenty-four hours after the Richardses had received their checks, their consciences were beginning to quiet down and grow discouraged; the elderly couple was learning to make peace with the sin they had committed. However, they were about to discover that a sin takes on new and genuine terrors when there appears to be a chance it might be discovered. This gives it a fresh and very real and significant dimension. At church that morning, the sermon followed the usual format; it contained the same familiar messages delivered in the same familiar manner; they had heard these words a thousand times and had always found them harmless, nearly meaningless, and easy to doze through; but today was different: the sermon seemed to be filled with accusations; it appeared to be directed straight and specifically at people who were hiding terrible sins. After the service, they escaped from the crowd of well-wishers as quickly as possible and rushed home, feeling chilled to their core by fears they couldn't identify—vague, shadowy, unclear anxieties. By chance, they spotted Mr. Burgess as he rounded a corner. He paid no attention to their acknowledging nod! He hadn't noticed it; but they didn't realize that. What could his behavior possibly mean? It might mean—it could—mean—oh, any number of terrible things. Was it possible that he knew Richards could have cleared him of wrongdoing in that past incident, and had been quietly waiting for an opportunity to settle the score? Once home, in their anxiety they began to imagine that their servant might have been in the adjoining room listening when Richards had revealed the secret to his wife about knowing of Burgess's innocence; then Richards started to imagine that he had heard the rustle of a dress in there at that moment; soon after, he was certain he had heard it. They decided to call Sarah in, using some excuse, and observe her expression; if she had been betraying them to Mr. Burgess, it would be evident in her behavior. They posed some questions to her—questions that were so scattered and disjointed and apparently pointless that the girl became convinced that the elderly couple's minds had been disturbed by their sudden wealth; the intense and suspicious stare they fixed upon her frightened her, and that sealed their suspicions. She turned red, became anxious and flustered, and to the old couple these were clear indicators of guilt—guilt of some dreadful kind or another—surely she was a spy and a betrayer. When they were alone once more, they started connecting many unrelated incidents and drawing horrible conclusions from these connections. When the situation had reached its worst point, Richards let out a sudden gasp and his wife asked:

"Oh, what is it?—what is it?"

"The note—Burgess's note! Its tone was sarcastic, I can see that now." He recited: "'Deep down you cannot respect me, knowing, as you do, about that matter I am accused of'—oh, it's completely clear now, God help me! He knows that I know! You can see how cleverly it was worded. It was a trap—and like an idiot, I fell right into it. And Mary—!"

"Oh, this is terrible—I know what you're going to say—he didn't give back your copy of the fake test comment."

"No—he kept it to destroy us with. Mary, he has already exposed us to some people. I know it—I know it well. I saw it in a dozen faces after church. Ah, he wouldn't acknowledge our nod of recognition—he knew what he had been doing!"

During the night, a doctor was summoned. Word spread the next morning that the elderly couple had fallen quite seriously ill—the physician explained they had been overwhelmed by the draining stress that came from their enormous stroke of luck, all the well-wishes from others, and staying up so late. The entire town felt genuinely upset by this news, since these two older residents were practically the only source of pride the community had remaining.

Two days later, the news had gotten worse. The elderly couple was delirious and behaving strangely. According to the nurses who witnessed it, Richards had been showing off checks—for $8,500? No—for an incredible amount of $38,500! What could possibly explain this enormous stroke of luck?

The next day the nurses brought more news—and it was wonderful. They had decided to hide the checks to keep them safe from harm, but when they looked for them, the checks had disappeared from under the patient's pillow—completely vanished. The patient said:

"Leave the pillow alone; what do you want?"

"We thought it would be best if the checks—"

"You will never see them again—they are destroyed. They came from Satan. I saw the mark of hell on them, and I knew they were sent to lead me into sin." Then he began rambling about strange and terrible things that were not clearly understandable, and which the doctor warned them to keep to themselves.

Richards was right; the checks were never seen again.

A nurse must have spoken while sleeping, because within two days the forbidden gossip had spread throughout the entire town, and the rumors were quite shocking. The talk suggested that Richards had actually been seeking the money bag for himself, and that Burgess had hidden this truth before spitefully revealing it.

Burgess was confronted with this accusation and firmly denied it. He argued that it wasn't fair to give credence to the rambling of a sick elderly man who had lost his mental faculties. Nevertheless, doubt lingered in the community, and people continued to discuss the matter extensively.

After a day or two, people began reporting that Mrs. Richards's delirious ramblings were starting to match her husband's exactly. Suspicion quickly turned into certainty, and the town's pride in having one remaining honest and respected citizen began to fade and move toward complete disappearance.

Six days went by, and then more news arrived. The elderly couple was dying. Richards's mind became clear in his final hour, and he asked for Burgess to come. Burgess said:

"Clear the room. I believe he wants to speak privately."

"No!" Richards declared; "I need witnesses. I want all of you to hear what I have to say, so I can die with dignity, not like some worthless creature. I was honest—on the surface—just like everyone else; and just like everyone else, I gave in when faced with temptation. I put my name to a lie and went after that wretched bag of money. Mr. Burgess recalled that I had helped him once, and out of appreciation (and not knowing the truth) he kept my claim quiet and protected me. You all remember what Burgess was accused of years back. Only my word, mine alone, could have proven his innocence, but I was too much of a coward and let him endure the shame—"

"No—no—Mr. Richards, you—"

"My servant betrayed my secret to him—"

"No one has betrayed anything to me—"

"And then he did something completely natural and understandable; he regretted the merciful kindness he had shown me, and he exposed me—just as I deserved—"

"Never! I swear it!"

"I forgive him from the bottom of my heart."

Burgess's passionate protests went unheard; the dying man passed away without realizing that he had wronged poor Burgess yet again. The old woman died that same night.

The final member of the sacred Nineteen had become a victim of the diabolical plundering; the town was robbed of the last remnant of its former magnificence. Its grief was not ostentatious, but it ran profound.

By an act of the Legislature—following a formal request and petition—Hadleyburg was permitted to change its name to (never mind what—I won't reveal it), and remove one word from the motto that had adorned the town's official seal for many generations.

The town has regained its integrity, and anyone hoping to catch it off guard again will need to get up very early in the morning.

THE END

Thank You For Reading

You've Just Read a Piece of the Greatest Library Ever Rebuilt

Thank you for reading.

This book is one of thousands we're restoring, reimagining, and translating as part of the **Modern Library of Alexandria** — a global movement to preserve and share humanity's most important ideas.

What was once lost to fire and time is now rising again — not just as memory, but as living, breathing knowledge, freely accessible to all.

What You Can Do Next:

- **Keep Reading.**

  Discover more legendary works — in beautiful print, audiobook, or digital form — at LibraryofAlexandria.com.

- **Build Your Own Library.**

  Every title is available as a paperback, hardcover, or collectible boxset — at true printing cost. Craft a personal library worthy of display.

- **Spread the Light.**

  Share this book. Tell others about the movement. Help us translate every timeless work into every language, so no reader is ever left behind.

By finishing this book, you've already taken part in something extraordinary.

Join us at LibraryofAlexandria.com

Together, we're rebuilding the greatest library the world has ever known.

With appreciation,

The Modern Library of Alexandria Team

Visit:
www.libraryofalexandria.com
Or scan the code below:

www.ingramcontent.com/pod-product-compliance
Lightning Source LLC
Chambersburg PA
CBHW012205030726
47494CB00022B/2357